an Angela Lindsey book

Printed in the United States of America.

Written by Angela Lindsey
Illustrated by Luis Peres

978-1-954893-02-3 Paperback
978-1-954893-00-9 Hardcover
978-1-954893-01-6 Ebook

Publisher's Cataloging-in-Publication data
Names: Lindsey, Angela, author. | Peres, Luis, illustrator.
Title: Silly Sam the Elf / by Angela Lindsey; illustrated by Luis Peres.
Description: Mechanicsville, MD: AMP Services, LLC, 2021. | Summary: Christmas Eve is here, and Santa's elves are busy making toys—all but Silly Sam, who is more interested in keeping the elves entertained. But when Sam tries on Santa's magical red suit, will he get the last laugh, or will Christmas be ruined?
Identifiers: LCCN: 2021915726 | ISBN: 978-1-954893-00-9 (hardcover) | 978-1-954893-02-3 (paperback) | 978-1-954893-01-6 (ebook)
Subjects: LCSH Elves--Juvenile fiction. | Santa Claus--Juvenile fiction. | Christmas stories. | CYAC Elves--Fiction. | Santa Claus--Fiction. | BISAC JUVENILE FICTION /Holidays & Celebrations / Christmas & Advent
Classification: LCC PZ7.1.L5585 Si 2021 | DDC [E]--dc23

This book belongs to:

____

Bobby, you are the best gift I have ever received.
I love watching you grow up and enjoy Christmas.
I can't believe your elves made it into a book!
You're so special and smart.
I am so proud of you always. Love, Mom.

Mom, you have passed your love of Christmas
down to all of your children and grandchildren.
I love your holiday countdowns and decorations.
I love the way you give all throughout the year.
Thank you for your support and love.
You're truly my best friend, always and forever.

Silly Sam
The Elf

Written by
Angela Lindsey

Illustrated by
Luis Peres

"I have the most special job in the world!" says Silly Sam.
"And I love making people laugh."

All his little elf life, Sam has dreamed of working with Santa. Now, finally, his dreams have come true.
As an elf in Santa 's toy shop, he gets to make all kinds of cool toys, like bikes, robots, and dollhouses.

On Christmas Eve, magic floats in the air.
The toy-maker elves are finishing up the toys.
The veterinary elves are taking care of the reindeer.
And the mechanical elves are making sure the sleigh is in perfect condition.
All over the North Pole, elves are singing as they work.

But Sam is not at his post.
He is up to his usual silliness.

jingle bells
RJL

Jingle bells, jingle bells
NORTH POLE

It makes Sam happy to know that his
work will bring joy to so many children.
But Sam likes to make the elves happy too.
He is always doing silly things to
make them laugh.
In fact, being silly is how he got
his nickname: Silly Sam!

Even on the busiest days,
Sam still finds time for silliness.
"Is everyone happy today?"
Sam asks the other elves.

Today, he does cartwheels
through the workshop, then
hands out cups of steaming
hot chocolate
topped with
reindeer-shaped
marshmallows.

The other elves all wear the sparkly red and green hats that Sam made for them.

"Santa, where are you?" shouts Sam as he opens the door to Santa's workshop. "I baked elf cookies just for you."

Sam peers around. Santa is nowhere to be seen, but hanging on a big hook is his magical red suit! "Ohhhh, what fun!" Sam whispers.

"I'm sure Santa won't mind if I just try it on for a minute."

Sam scrambles into the suit, which—of course—is way too big.

Then he has a silly idea. "I 'll just stuff this suit a bit," he says. Into the suit go fluffy Rudolphs and Grinches , along with teddy bears, snowmen, and gingerbread men.

He even adds a pillow that's shaped like a peppermint candy.

That's when the magic begins to happen.

Suddenly, the stuffed animals POP out of the suit and back onto the shelves.
Looking down, Sam sees that he's turned into Santa!
"Woah. Cool!" Sam shrieks.

Laughing, he races off to show
his friends Elfsana and Elfie how
silly and special he looks
in Santa 's suit.

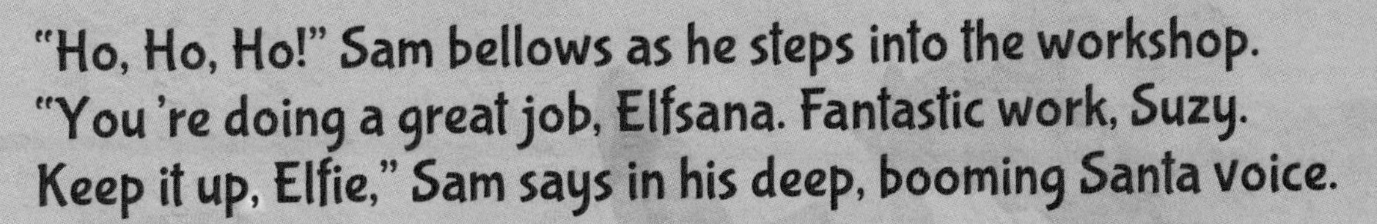

"Ho, Ho, Ho!" Sam bellows as he steps into the workshop. "You 're doing a great job, Elfsana. Fantastic work, Suzy. Keep it up, Elfie," Sam says in his deep, booming Santa voice.

Elfsana blushes. "Thank you, Santa."

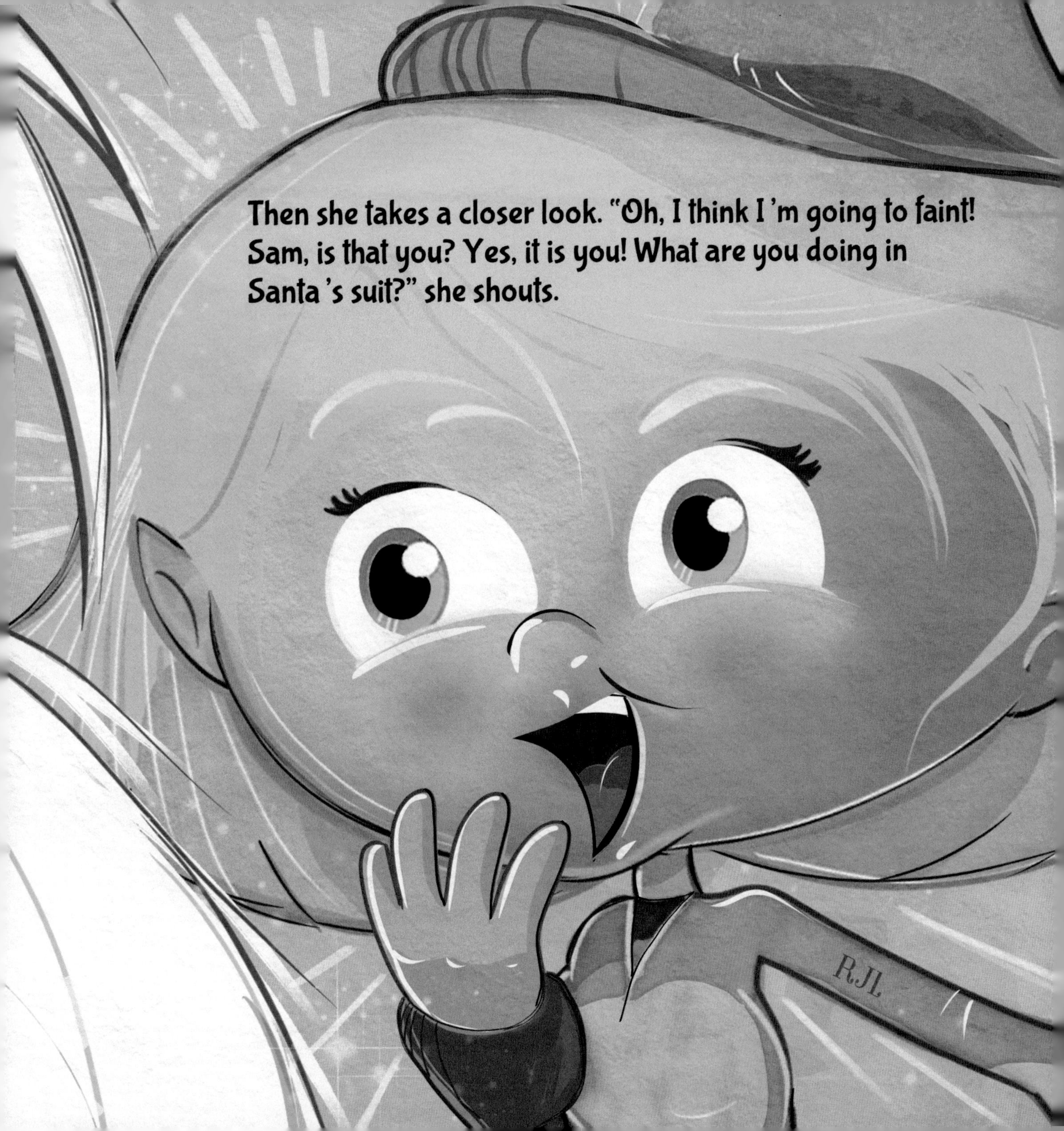

Then she takes a closer look. "Oh, I think I 'm going to faint! Sam, is that you? Yes, it is you! What are you doing in Santa 's suit?" she shouts.

"You 're stealing Santa 's magic!
Take that suit off quickly.
You are going to be
in so much trouble!"

"But . . ." Sam starts.

Then a rumbly feeling takes over his belly. What if Elfsana is right? Is he stealing Santa's magic?

Sam starts to take off the suit, but it's too late.
A loud, jolly laugh fills the room.

Looking up, Sam finds himself
face-to-face with Santa.
"Hi, Santa," he squeaks.

"So this is where my suit went," Santa says thoughtfully.

Sam tries to explain. "I 'm sorry, Santa. I was just being silly. I wanted to be like you and make everyone happy.

No one ever told me that putting on your suit takes away your magic. Does this mean that I 'm Santa now?"

"Oh, no," Santa says. "My magic can never be taken away. But the suit is magical, and putting it on did give you special powers. I'm still Santa, but it seems you now have a little magic from the suit."

For the first time, Sam doesn ’t feel silly. He feels scared. “Are you disappointed in me?” he whispers.

Santa lets out a big belly laugh. “Ho, ho, ho. No, no, no, Sam. I know you were just being silly. You just wanted to make the other elves smile.

But I need the magic you drew from the suit to help me deliver all the toys around the world. That means I need you.”

"How would you like
to join me on my
sleigh tonight?"

"Me?" Sam asks, his heart filling with joy.
"Come with YOU and the reindeer to
DELIVER THE TOYS? Yes! Yes! Yes!
I mean thank you, Santa.
I would be honored."

R.J.

Away! Off they go, headed for the most marvelous night of Sam 's life. As they fly through the starry night sky, Sam looks over the edge in awe, watching the moonlit rivers and oceans and the snow-covered houses passing below. Christmas Eve dazzle lights up the sky.

RJL

Sam hears children's prayers floating up through the clouds as the children try to fall asleep so Santa can arrive.

Jingle bells, jingle bells
All night, Sam and Santa deliver toys.
Ho, Ho, Ho!
RJL

As the sun rises, the two touch down at the North Pole.

"Thank you, Santa," Sam says.

"Thank you for this magical night. I will never forget it. And I'm sorry about the suit."

"Thank YOU, Sam,"
Santa says with a twinkle
in his eye.
"For reminding me that
Christmas is a time to
be together!

You are a good elf, and
I am lucky that
you are the one
who got his
hands on
the suit."

Sam smiles. "I promise never to touch it again. But how will you keep anyone else from touching it?"
At that, Santa 's face grows serious.

"I don 't know, Sam. I just don 't know."

"Hmmm, a master elf," Santa says thoughtfully. "A master elf. Why, yes, that might be just the thing." And with that, Santa disappears, off to prepare for next year.

"A master elf," Sam whispers to himself. "I wonder who it will be."

R.J.L.
the end

ABOUT THE AUTHOR

Angela Lindsey

Angela Lindsey is the award-winning, best-selling author of the *Waverly the Witch* series, and she has more books on the way. A proud mom of one, Angela enjoys telling fun and inventive stories, taking inspiration from her son, Bobby, her husband, Robert, and their many family adventures.

When Angela isn't writing, she spends her time running businesses, volunteering at shelters and school events, and advocating for chronic illness patients like herself. She is proud of her religious faith, and she values family above all. Angela enjoys reading books, watching movies, spending time at the beach, and hosting parties for friends and family.

Angela plans to continue her writing journey and has many new publishing projects in the works. Fans can stay up to date with Angela's books by visiting www.angelalindsey.com.